# Good-Night,  Owl!

FOR MORGAN'S GRANDPA

GOOD-
OWL!

PAT HUTCHINS

## PUFFIN BOOKS

*in association with The Bodley Head*

Owl tried to sleep.

The bees buzzed,
buzz buzz,
and Owl tried to sleep.

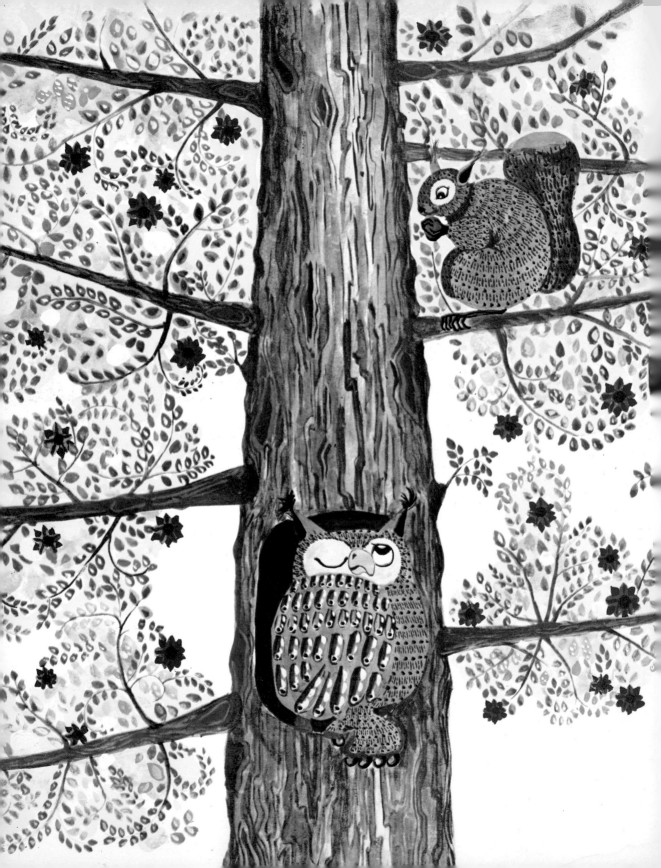

The squirrel cracked nuts,
crunch crunch,
and Owl tried to sleep.

The crows croaked,
caw caw,
and Owl tried to sleep.

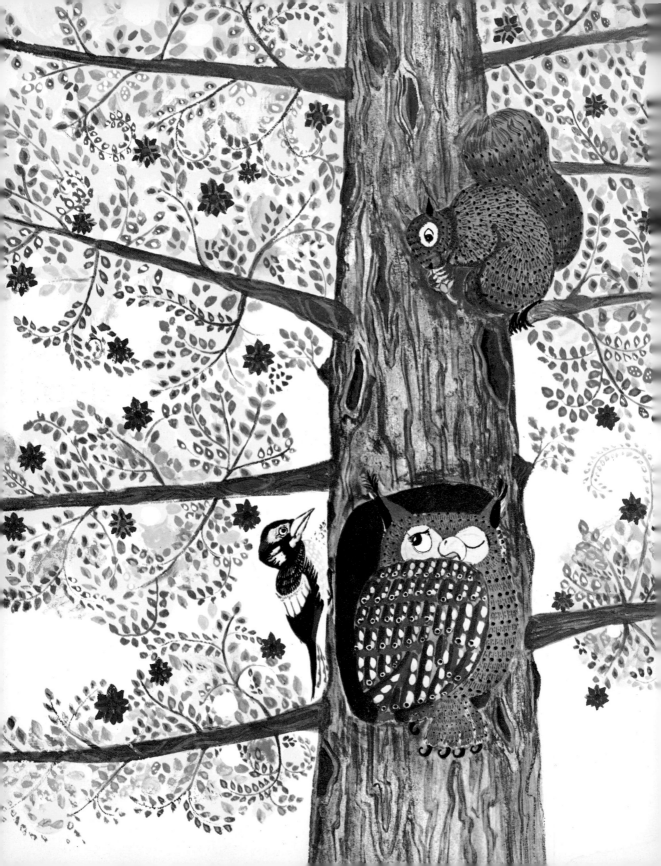

The woodpecker pecked,
rat-a-tat! rat-a-tat!
and Owl tried to sleep.

The starlings chittered
twit-twit, twit-twit
and Owl tried to sleep.

The jays screamed,
ark ark,
and Owl tried to sleep.

The cuckoo called,
cuckoo cuckoo,
and Owl tried to sleep.

The robin peeped,
        pip pip,
and Owl tried to sleep.

The sparrows chirped,
cheep cheep,
and Owl tried to sleep.

The doves cooed,
croo croo,
and Owl tried to sleep.

The bees buzzed, buzz buzz.
The squirrel cracked nuts,
crunch crunch.
The crows croaked, caw caw.
The woodpecker pecked,
rat-a-tat! rat-a-tat!
The starlings chittered,
twit-twit, twit-twit.
The jays screamed, ark ark.
The cuckoo called,
cuckoo cuckoo.
The robin peeped, pip pip.
The sparrows chirped,
cheep cheep.
The doves cooed, croo croo,
and Owl couldn't sleep.

Then darkness fell
and the moon came up.
And there wasn't a sound.

Owl screeched,
screech screech,
and woke everyone up.

**www.heinemannlibrary.co.uk**
Visit our website to find out more information about Heinemann Library books.

To order:
☎ Phone 44 (0) 1865 888066
🖹 Send a fax to 44 (0) 1865 314091
💻 Visit the Heinemann Bookshop at www.heinemannlibrary.co.uk to browse our catalogue and order online.

Heinemann Library is an imprint of Capstone Global Library Limited, a company incorporated in England and Wales having its registered office at 7 Pilgrim Street, London, EC4V 6LB – Registered company number: 6695582

Heinemann is a registered trademark of Pearson Education Limited, under licence to Capstone Global Library Limited

Edited by Siân Smith, Rebecca Rissman, and Charlotte Guillain
Designed by Joanna Hinton-Malivoire
Picture research by Tracy Cummins and Heather Mauldin
Production by Duncan Gilbert
Originated by Heinemann Library
Printed and bound in China by South China Printing Company Ltd

ISBN 978 0 431 02042 6
13 12 11 10 09
 0 9 8 7 6 5 4 3 2 1

**British Library Cataloguing in Publication Data**
Guillain, Charlotte
   The Sun. - (Space)
   1. Sun - Juvenile literature
   I. Title
   523.7

**Acknowledgements**
We would like to thank the following for permission to reproduce photographs: Getty Images pp. **5** (©Panoramic Images), **6** (©Guy Edwardes), **7** (©Tohoku Color Agency), **9** (©Stocktrek Images), **14** (©William Radcliffe), **17** (©Smari), **18** (©DAJ), **19** (©Scott Stulberg), **22** (©Smari); NASA pp. **4**, **8**, **10**, **23a**, **23b** (©SOHO); Photo Researchers Inc pp.**11** (©M. Kulyk), **13** (©Roger Harris), **15** (©Detlev van Ravenswaay), **21** (©Mark Garlick); Shutterstock pp.**12** (©Sebastian Kaulitzki), **20** (©Hashim Pudiyapura), **23c** (©Sebastian Kaulitzki).

Front cover photograph reproduced with permission of NASA (©SOHO). Back cover photograph reproduced with permission of Shutterstock (©Sebastian Kaulitzki).

Every effort has been made to contact copyright holders of material reproduced in this book. Any omissions will be rectified in subsequent printings if notice is given to the publishers.

Space

# The Sun

## Charlotte Guillain

Heinemann
LIBRARY

# Contents

# The Sun

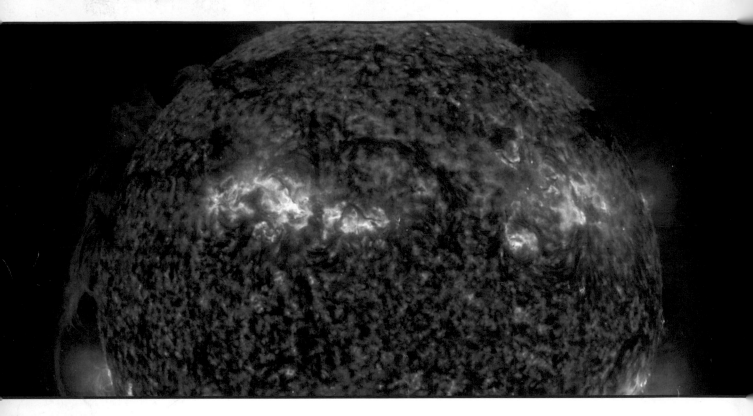

The Sun is in space.

Space is up above the sky.

5

# What is the Sun like?

The Sun is a star.

The Sun is much closer to us than other stars.

The Sun is a giant ball of gas.

The Sun is very hot and bright.

9

The Sun is made of layers.

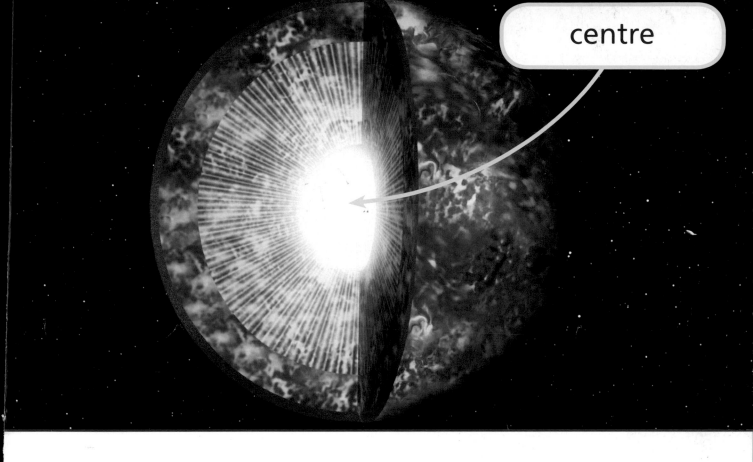

centre

The Sun is hottest in the centre.

# The Solar System

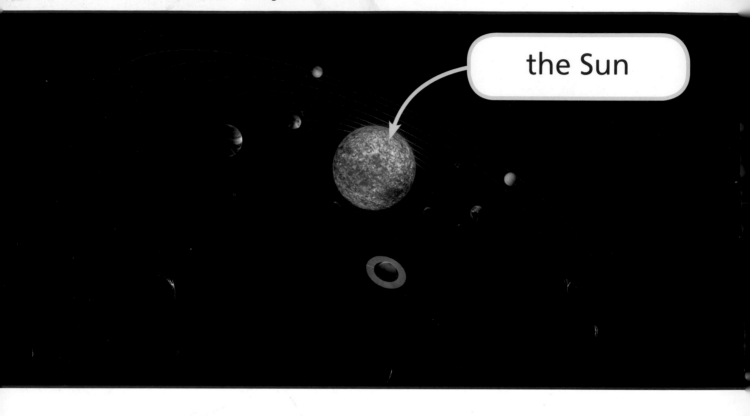

the Sun

The Sun and the planets around it are called the Solar System.

The planets move around, or orbit,
the Sun.

13

The Sun gives the planets heat.

14

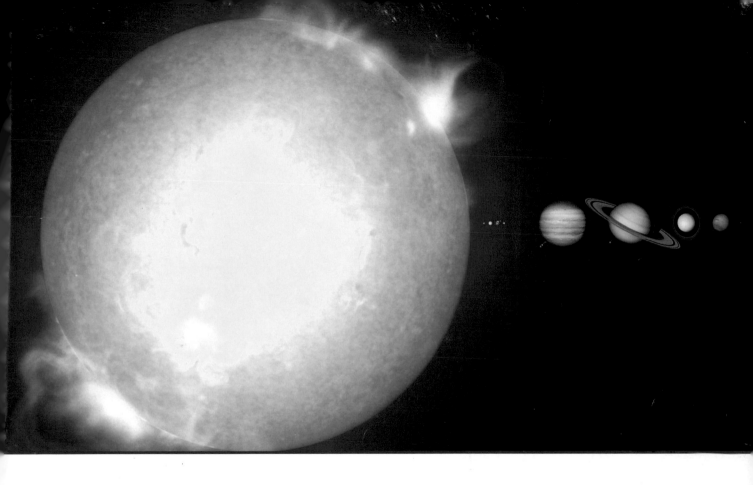

The Sun gives the planets light.

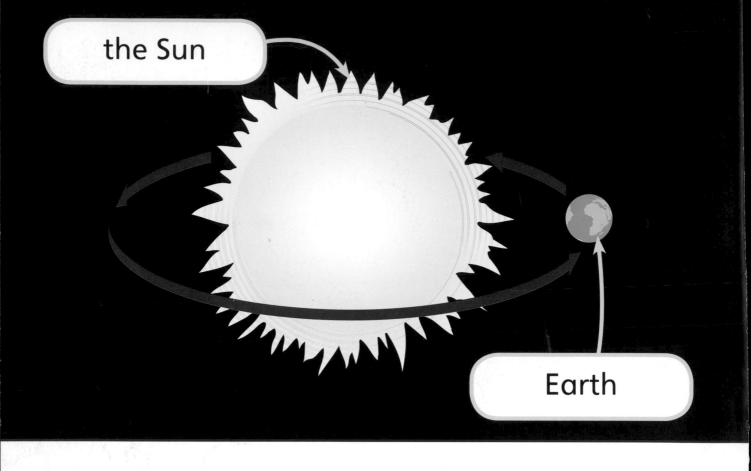

the Sun

Earth

Earth orbits the Sun.

Living things on Earth need the Sun.

The Sun gives living things light.

The Sun gives living things heat.

# The Moon

The Moon does not make its own light.

the Moon

the Sun

Light from the Sun makes the
Moon shine.

# Can you remember?

## Why do living things need the Sun?

22

Answer on p.24

# Picture glossary

**gas** not solid like wood or liquid like water. Air is a gas that we breathe in but cannot see.

**layer** when something has layers it is made up of different parts that lie on top of each other

**orbit** move around

**Solar System** the name for the Sun and the eight planets that move around it

# Index

Answer to question on p.22: Living things need the Sun for light and heat.

**Notes for parents and teachers**

**Before reading**

Ask the children what they think the Sun gives us on Earth (heat and light). Explain that the Sun is an enormous ball of extremely hot gas in the sky. We need heat and light from the Sun but we have to be careful too. Talk to the children about using sun cream and wearing a hat in sunny weather. Caution them about never looking directly at the sun.

**After reading**

• Make a paper plate sun. You will need a paper plate for each child. Tell them to paint the back of the plate with yellow paint. They should trace around their hand seven times. Cut out the hands and paint them yellow. Glue or staple the hands to the paper plate to make the Sun's rays.

• Make a sundial. You will need a stick approximately 30cm long. Fix the stick in the middle of an old plate using play dough. Place the stick and plate in a sunny spot in the playground. At every hour, put a small pebble to mark where the shadow of the stick falls. (Note: It may take a few days to get pebbles for each hour.) When you have a marker for each hour, talk to the children about telling the time using the sundial.